The Case of the
Burgled
Blessing Box

Books by Scott Corbett

The Case of the Burgled Blessing Box

by Scott Corbett

Illustrated by Paul Frame

An Atlantic Monthly Press Book

BOSTON   Little, Brown and Company   TORONTO

FIRST EDITION

T10/75

Library of Congress Cataloging in Publication Data

Corbett, Scott.
   The case of the burgled blessing box.

"An Atlantic Monthly Press book."
   SUMMARY: Twelve-year-old Inspector Tearle investigates
the missing receipts of a revivalist religious group.
   [1. Mystery and detective stories. 2. Revivals—
Fiction] I. Frame, Paul. II. Title.
PZ7.C79938Cam   [Fic]   75–15915
ISBN 0–316–15724–4

ATLANTIC–LITTLE, BROWN BOOKS
ARE PUBLISHED BY
LITTLE, BROWN AND COMPANY
IN ASSOCIATION WITH
THE ATLANTIC MONTHLY PRESS

Published simultaneously in Canada
by Little, Brown & Company (Canada) Limited

PRINTED IN THE UNITED STATES OF AMERICA

U. S. 1881989

To

Merlyn Townley

The Case of the Burgled Blessing Box

One

SLUMPED IN HIS CHAIR with his feet on his desk, Inspector Tearle lamented the passing of summer. The golden days were almost at an end, the confinements of school about to return.

Life was running down. Nothing was happening anywhere. The only special event about to take place on the local scene was a revival meeting over at the county fairgrounds, and Roger did not feel like having his soul saved by some fire-breathing preacher.

He looked about him at his desk, his two-drawer steel filing cabinet, and his telephone. All too soon now, they would be gone. With the help of his sister Shirley and their best friend Thumbs Thorndyke, he would have to move his office inside for the winter. Not until another summer rolled around would he again enjoy the distinction of being (he felt sure) the only twelve-year-old detective who had an office in a tree house.

And a genuine detective he was. He had framed letters of commendation from Colonel Dougherty of the State Police hanging on his bedroom wall to prove it. He had won his nickname of "Inspector" by hard service in the field. The past months had provided not only some astonishing cases, but also the free time to pursue them. But now summer was nearly over, and soon —

The telephone squawked.

His private line, which he had personally installed, ran over to the house and down to a kitchen window. Expecting a summons to dinner, Roger answered in a falsetto, "Inspector Tearle's office, Miss Widget speaking."

"Roger! Guess what?" Shirley was giggling wildly. "Mom went to school with Angel Rose!"

"What? You mean that singer who —"

"Yes! The one with that revival preacher, Reverend What's-his-name!"

"Buddy Joe Billings," said Roger, who made a practice of remembering names, as any good detective should.

"That's right! Mom just opened up the paper with their picture in it and said, 'Why, that's Rose Hartwick, we went to school together! She won All-State Cheerleader when we were in high school!' "

Roger's eyebrows and eyes and mouth, all of which turned down at the corners, made him look mournful even when he was his normal, cheerful self. When he was really feeling melancholy, as now, he looked as woebegone as a cat that has just lost its eighth life and is skating on thin ice. But as he listened to Shirley's news a grin split the mournful look to smithereens.

"I'll be right in," he said.

Swarming down the ladder in a way that emphasized his bony legs and arms and made him seem all knees and elbows, Roger hurried into the kitchen to join the family circle. His father's and sister's faces wore wide grins. His mother's had the defensive look of someone who is being unmercifully teased.

"Now, Roger, don't *you* start in," she said, but Roger started in anyway.

"My gosh, I hope we can keep this a secret. If it ever gets around East Widmarsh that *my* mother went to school with anyone called Angel Rose — !"

"She wasn't called that then, she was plain Rose," Mrs. Tearle retorted. "Well, I shouldn't say plain, because she was the class beauty — and she's still got her looks, even though she's put on a little weight."

The newspaper was lying on the kitchen table, opened to a four-column picture of three people. In the center was a stocky, round-faced man with short gray hair and eyes like searchlights, who looked as if he had a ruddy complexion. On his left was a broad-shouldered young man with dark wavy hair and enough large, brilliant teeth to fit out four movie stars. On his right was a woman . . .

Well, she certainly had a beautiful face, and she was

not fat, but she was undeniably large and plentiful. She was abundantly curved, her long blond hair was a cascade of ringlets, and she looked as if she were full of life. Together the three of them exuded enough vitality, even in a news photo, to make anyone feel worn out just looking at them.

The caption identified them as "Rev. Buddy Joe Billings (center) with Brother Leroy Mason and Angel Rose." The story under the picture was headlined, FOUR-DAY REVIVAL BEGINS AT FAIRGROUNDS.

"I wish I had a nickel for every time I've turned off their radio program on Sunday morning," said Mr. Tearle.

"And to think, that soprano who's always singing in the background when the program starts is my old schoolmate and I didn't even know it!" cried Mrs. Tearle.

"All-State Cheerleader, sis-boom-bah!" cried Roger.

"She was also the star of the glee club," his mother informed him with great dignity. "She had a lovely voice, even then. Rose Hartwick! I can't get over it. I wonder how she ever got into — into religion?" she added, groping for a term. "Of course, she was a soloist in church choirs, too, but —"

Mrs. Tearle paused, and looked at her husband with a determined expression.

"Well, I can tell you one thing, Jim," she said. "*I'm* going over there tonight to see Rose!"

She spoke as though she expected opposition, but he only grinned.

"Well, I can tell you another thing, Enid," he said. "I never thought anything would get me inside a revival tent — but I wouldn't miss this meeting for anything!"

"Me, either!" said Shirley. "Call up Thumbs, Roger. I'll bet he'd like to come, too."

"I hope so," snapped Mrs. Tearle. "It will be nice to have *one* gentleman along!"

The fairgrounds were four miles from the village of East Widmarsh on the road to Burgessville. They arrived early, the idea being that if Mrs. Tearle could see Angel Rose before the meeting began she would ask her to come home with them afterward.

Early as they were, there were already a few cars in the parking lot in front of the big tent. The tent's sidewalls were rolled up to keep it airy, and a sharp glow slanted out from its brightly lighted interior into the soft dusk of early evening. Two men were puttering around outside, checking guy ropes. The melody of a relatively cheerful hymn indicated that someone inside was making sure the electric organ was in good working order. Floodlights illuminated the banner that arched across the front of the tent, a banner on which the words "Spread the Light" glittered in gold.

Mr. Tearle asked the two men where they might find Angel Rose. One blinked at him with pale, watery old eyes and said, "Well, she's probably getting ready for the meeting. I don't know as she could have any visitors . . ."

"My wife went to school with her."

"Oh." The watery eyes swam back and forth from face to face, taking them all in, and then he said, "Well, I guess that's different. Walk back alongside the tent, she's in the camper nearest the office."

Out behind the tent they found five vehicles parked in a semicircle. One looked like a moving van, one like a converted bus, and three were identical campers. The whole fleet was painted white, and each vehicle's side carried the words "Spread the Light" in letters of gold. Mr. Tearle pointed to the bus.

"That must be their office, so let's try that first camper."

He tapped on the door. They waited. Then suddenly it was flung open and a woman stood in the doorway in a flowing white robe with dazzling light behind her. At that instant she did indeed look like an angel — a large and startling angel. But almost in the same instant, after a single stare at Mrs. Tearle, her face lighted up with recognition.

"Why, as I live and breathe, it's Enid Weatherby!" she cried, and stepped outside. Mrs. Tearle disappeared into the folds of the white robes as they hugged each other with a giggling ecstasy that must have been reserved for old schoolmates.

When everybody had been introduced and Angel Rose

9

had kissed everybody in sight before they knew what hit them, Mrs. Tearle said, "I know you haven't much time right now, but I wanted to see if you could come back with us for dessert and coffee after your meeting."

"I'd love to! But listen, I've got a few minutes right now, too, so come on in, you and Jim — you kids don't mind? — there's not room enough for all of us —"

"We'll walk around," said Roger, glad enough not to be one of six packed into a small space with such a human dynamo.

They walked away with straight faces. Not until the camper's door had safely closed did they begin to grin at each other.

"Wow!" said Thumbs.

"No wonder she was All-State Cheerleader!" said Shirley.

"Poor Mom!" said Roger. "She'll never hear the end of this."

As usual, Inspector Tearle made a thorough survey of his surroundings. First came a quick estimate of the seating capacity of the tent — about eight hundred, according to his calculations. Two aisles divided the folding chairs into a center section and two side sections. On each chair was a leaflet. He examined one and found it contained a message of welcome, the words of several familiar hymns, and some information about the Sunday radio program. Oh, yes, and a form on which to make a pledge, for those who cared to do so.

Organ music was now being provided steadily by a young man they recognized as Brother Leroy. Quite a sprinkling of early-comers were scattered around the tent, fanning themselves with their leaflets, and Brother Leroy treated them to a display of his magnificent teeth from time to time as he played.

What with one thing and another it was a while before the sightseers returned to Angel Rose's camper. As they approached, the door opened and she beckoned to them.

"Hi, there! Your folks just left. Come in here a minute, I want to talk to you."

Surprised but curious, Roger said, "Yes, ma'am," and in they went.

The camper's space was not cramped, but even so, with Angel Rose present it seemed as if there were a good many of them inside. She looked at Roger with an odd expression, as though she were seeing him for the first time.

"Roger, your folks tell me you're quite a detective, even had letters from the head of the State Police," she began briskly. "You must have handled yourself pretty well."

"Well, I —"

"You stand pretty high with the police."

"Well, they —"

"I mean, they'd take your word for it, if you said something was so?"

"Well, yes, I suppose —"

"Praise the Lord," breathed Angel Rose. "I think He's sent me exactly what I need!"

Two

INSPECTOR TEARLE FOUND this suggestion of divine intervention stirring but confusing. What had he been sent for?

"Well, I —"

"Something funny's going on around here, something we need help to check up on," said Angel Rose, "and it suddenly came to me that the very people who could do the job without making anyone suspicious would be — kids! The right kids, of course, and you're just the ones. Friends of an old school chum of mine — why, nobody will think a thing about it! Now, I haven't got time to go into it now, but I'll tell you all about it when we get back to your house."

"Okay! But whatever it is, be sure not to make it sound dangerous, or we'll have trouble with Mom."

"Oh, it won't be *dangerous*, but it may get exciting —

and you'll be doing work for the Lord! Now, run along, and we'll talk about it later!"

Under the broad spread of the brightly lighted tent sat row upon row of people, and the "Amens!" and "Hallelujahs!" were coming thick and fast as the short, burly figure on the platform in front of them waved his arms and rolled out his message in a bullhorn voice. Roger had not heard anything like it since old Miss Gideon had stopped teaching Sunday school, and even she had not been as quick with the Scriptures as this man was.

"There was a time, brothers and sisters, yes, there was a time when Judah and Israel dwelt safely, every man under his vine and under his fig tree, but then there came a time when there was no king in Israel, when every man did that which was right in his own eyes," boomed the Reverend Buddy Joe, and stabbed a blunt finger at his audience. "I tell you, that's where we've got to now, and we've got to get back to God. I have seen the wicked in great power, and spreading himself like a green bay tree, but I say to you the righteous shall flourish, he shall grow like a cedar in Lebanon, and that's the path for you and me to follow . . ."

Every time he quoted from the Bible the Reverend Buddy Joe's voice seemed to put quotation marks around the words. When he spoke about the righteous flourishing, and some Bible student in the crowd got carried away and shouted, "Ninety-second Psalm, O Lord!,"

Buddy Joe picked him right up with, "That's right, brother, those golden words are straight out of the ninety-second Psalm, verse twelve, and that's only one of one hundred and fifty golden psalms we all ought to be reading and rereading every day of our lives!"

"How's that for fast fielding?" Roger whispered admiringly to Thumbs.

"Had him out at first by a mile," Thumbs agreed.

It was a wonder that Roger even followed the exchange because he was trying to watch everything and everyone at once. A new case had been dumped into his lap; it was hard to think of anything else. If, as Angel Rose had said, something funny was going on, what might it be? With Inspector Tearle, curiosity was an occupational disease, and she had aroused it to fever pitch. He sought eagerly for something that would give him a hint.

Flanking the Reverend Buddy Joe on the platform were his two assistants. To his left stood Brother Leroy in front of the electric organ he played whenever Angel Rose sang or their leader encouraged the audience to join in on a familiar hymn. To his right stood Angel Rose, radiant in her long white robe. On a rainbow arch above the platform glittered the revivalist's message in more letters of gold, SPREAD THE LIGHT.

When the meeting started, the Reverend Buddy Joe was wearing a black coat and tie that gave him a definitely clerical look, but after he had warmed up and started what he called "pitching in for the Lord," he took off his coat, loosened his tie, and rolled up his sleeves, all of which actions drew noisy approval from the crowd.

After a while it became evident that the Reverend Buddy Joe's thoughts were turning to the question of the collection. Appropriate references from the Scriptures began to be woven into his talk.

"He that giveth to the poor shall not lack. . . . Cast thy bread upon the waters: for thou shalt find it after many days. . . . For thou has been a strength to the poor, a strength to the needy in his distress. . . . What man is

there of you, whom if his son ask bread, will give him a stone? . . ."

Finally he got down to specifics.

"Now, friends, you know the good work we're doing to Spread the Light, and you know that in this world of ours it takes money to do that. You all know about the Gospel College we've started back at our headquarters in Oklahoma, where already nearly a hundred fine young men and women are learning how to go forth and Spread the Light so that the Good News I'm bringing you tonight can be carried to the four corners of the earth — and you know that takes money! Not to mention what it costs us to put our radio hour on ninety-three stations from coast to coast!

"So now, I want you to take a bill out of your pocket — a dollar bill, or a five-dollar bill, a ten or even a *twenty* — whatever you have and know in your heart you ought to give — and I want you to close your eyes and press your fingers hard on that bill and say a special prayer before you put it into one of our old-fashioned collection bags, because I want you to know that after you have left here and gone home I will do the same thing, I'll hold each and every one of your hard-earned bills in my hand one by one and bless them one by one, and I'll feel your touch joined to my touch, and together we'll ask the Lord to answer your prayer!"

These words, uttered with fierce conviction, were obviously effective. All through the tent the rustle of paper money could be heard as people got their offerings ready. Looking around him, Roger saw that at least three-quarters of the audience did indeed have their eyes closed and seemed to be praying as they clutched their bills. Here and there he spotted tens and twenties — generally held a little higher than necessary, it seemed to him, else why were they so noticeable?

His father whispered into his ear as he gave Roger a glimpse of a ten-dollar bill, "What do you say to two bucks a head?"

"Sounds fair enough to me," said Roger.

"Can't let your mother's old cheerleader down — especially when it looks like she's going to help take up the collection personally."

While the Reverend Buddy Joe's words streamed on, Brother Leroy and Angel Rose had left the platform and joined three men whom the preacher had introduced earlier as his "trusted helpers, Homer, Pete, and Floyd" — Homer was the one with the watery eyes.

All five of them had deftly possessed themselves of long-handled collection bags with which to reach in from the aisles and had begun the collection with the precision of a team, each taking a certain section of the audience. The three trusted helpers were all small, stringy, weatherbeaten older men who looked as if they had seen worse times. Homer and Pete were the men Mr. Tearle had spoken to when they were looking for Angel Rose.

When the collection was completed the collectors disappeared smoothly into a curtained-off section at the rear of the tent, unnoticed by most of the crowd except Roger, and the Reverend Buddy Joe was left with the platform to himself.

Now he began to talk about the Light, and what the Light meant to all of them. And as he talked, the lights in the tent gradually grew dimmer, ever so slowly dimmer. Roger noticed that the sidewalls of the tent were being rolled down, section by section, though no one in the spellbound audience seemed aware of it.

His face shining with purpose and perspiration, the Reverend Buddy Joe threw himself into the work of the Lord, and he was good at it. The searchlight eyes swept his listeners like beacons; the atmosphere in the tent was alive and tingling with his vitality. He had that mysterious, electric quality that projected itself toward every person present and made every one of them feel he was being spoken to personally.

"Friends, I want you to understand what Light means, what it means to all of us, so I'm going to take you on a journey into the dark. But be not afraid, for God is with us!"

All at once the tent was pitch dark. And out of the darkness came the preacher's voice solemnly booming the opening words of the Bible:

"In the beginning God created the heaven and the earth.

"And the earth was without form, and void; and darkness was upon the face of the deep. And the Spirit of God moved upon the face of the waters.

"And God said, 'Let there be light': *and there was light.*"

Light! As the final word thundered, the lights came on again, full, brilliant, and dazzling, and the organ sounded, and Angel Rose sang "Hallelujah!" in a voice that would have shattered a goblet. There they were, she and Brother Leroy, miraculously back in their places.

The effect was powerful, no doubt about it, and the Reverend Buddy Joe had his audience with him as he stepped forward and spread his arms and cried, "What better work can we do, brethren, than to Spread the Light?"

Three

Even when she had exchanged her flowing white robe for a summery print dress, Angel Rose still seemed to Spread the Light.

The fair complexion of her face, with only the tiniest beginning of a double chin beneath it to suggest she should watch her calories, glowed with light. Her pearly teeth gleamed. Her long blond hair shimmered and her blue eyes sparkled. She remained overwhelming.

Chocolate cake and ice cream rated high on Inspector Tearle's list of dessert favorites, but he had trouble concentrating on them that night. Their visitor had firmly postponed explaining what was on her mind until after they had given the dessert its due. And she did her part with a gusto that amounted almost to greed. But then, at last, when the six plates were empty, she turned to Mrs. Tearle and began.

"Enid, did Roger tell you about the conversation we had before the meeting started?"

"Why, no," said Mrs. Tearle.

"I figured I'd wait to let you explain," said Roger, and he received a nod of approval from Angel Rose.

"That shows good sense," she said. "Makes me surer than ever you were sent on purpose."

Mrs. Tearle looked understandably mystified and, knowing her son, instantly concerned.

"Sent for what, Rose?"

Angel Rose leaned forward and swiveled a solemn glance around the table.

"What I'm going to tell you must not leave this room. Can I depend on that?"

Mr. Tearle chuckled wryly.

"Well, if anyone can keep a secret, it's these three kids."

"They've even kept a few from *us* on certain occasions," said Mrs. Tearle, giving her son a sharp glance.

"Only when absolutely necessary," said Inspector Tearle.

Angel Rose leaned back with a satisfied expression.

"I knew I was right about you, all of you. Well, now. You know what you were telling me, Enid — about those letters Roger got from the head of the State Police, and all? That's what started me thinking. Because we've got a problem, a real bad one. Something funny is going on, and it has me worried sick.

"It has to do with the collection.

"After the collection is finished, Brother Leroy and I

take all the bags out to the office. Homer has to stay in the back end of the tent to manage the lights. Pete and Floyd roll down the sidewalls and then stand by with flashlights in case anything should go wrong.

"What we call our office is that big old bus — it used to be a bus, that is, but we've fitted it out as an office, and Pete and Floyd sleep in there nights, too. Homer sleeps in the van that carries all our equipment.

"Inside the office on a table is the Blessing Box. That's what we empty all the money into. And that's where we leave it. We lock the door, but that's all we do. I've always felt the money ought to go straight into the safe, but B.J. won't hear of it — that's what we call the Reverend for short, B.J. He says the Blessing Box is sacred, and nobody's going to touch it. And he's been right — until lately, that is.

"Anyway, after we lock up, Brother Leroy and I wait till the lights go out in the tent. The minute they go out we hurry back and quietly get into place on the platform, ready for when the lights come on again.

"After the meeting is over, B.J. blesses the money, just like he says. He goes into the office alone and blesses every last bill of it, one by one. He also counts it. When he's finished, he puts the money in a little safe we have and brings me a slip of paper with the total on it, because I keep the books. The next day one of us takes the money to a bank and gets a bank check to send home to our headquarters.

"But for some time now it has seemed to Brother Leroy and me that the collections haven't been quite what they should be. You get so you can judge pretty close, and it just seemed to us . . . Well, to make a long story short, one night we decided to count the money.

"We were ashamed of ourselves, doing a thing like that, but we felt we had to do *something* — so we counted it. And I can tell you we had to count fast, because we only had about five minutes before we had to be back in the tent. But we got the money counted, dumped it in the Blessing Box, and got back to the tent in time.

"Sure enough, when B.J. gave me his count that night, there was well over a hundred dollars' difference between what we counted and what he counted!"

Angel Rose paused to stare around at them with a stricken expression.

"Well, I'll be a —" Mr. Tearle began, and then thought better of what he would be. "You mean to say that B.J. —"

"Heavens, no!" Angel Rose threw up her hands in pious protest. "Nothing could make me believe that holy man would take anything extra for himself. He limits himself to a small salary, same as the rest of us — it's not near as much as some people might think, but — No, it's got to be that someone else is getting at that money between the time we leave the office and the time B.J. goes in. Now, of course, the thing I'm hoping is that it's

24

some outsider doing it, someone who's decided he's onto a good thing and is following us from town to town."

Roger the Boy Bloodhound, as he was also sometimes called, was already sniffing intently at the trail as Angel Rose described the routine. But no whiff of an outsider reached his nostrils.

"The collection must amount to quite a bit," he remarked, trying to be delicate about it. But Angel Rose spoke frankly.

"It'll run to several thousand dollars some nights," she told them. "Now, tonight was a light night — I don't suppose there were more than five hundred souls on hand — but we expected that. This is one of our trouble spots. I don't mean to criticize, but your neighbors around this area have been slow to see the Light. Why, would you believe it, the Burgessville radio station is threatening to drop our Sunday morning hour! Well, that's a challenge B.J. wasn't about to take lying down, so that's why we came here. Why, in the right places we've drawn flocks of two and three thousand a night!"

"Hmm. If that's the case," Mr. Tearle put in, "I can't imagine some thief trailing all over the country after you and taking chances night after night, just to skim off a hundred bucks or so at a time, when he could make one grab and get away with thousands."

Roger listened approvingly. Exactly what he had been thinking. Angel Rose sighed.

"I suppose you're right, but I can't help doing some

wishful thinking, because that way would be so much nicer than having it be one of our own."

"I can understand your feelings, but from the sound of it, it has to be an inside job," said Mr. Tearle. "Now, what about those three helpers?"

"Homer and Pete and Floyd? Why, it's hard for me to believe that any of those devoted men, after all B.J.'s done for them, and however sorely tempted they might be, could ever . . . could ever . . . Before they saw the Light, poor Homer was an alcoholic. Pete has done more time in jail than you kids are old and Floyd was a small-time confidence man. But even so, I just can't believe that they . . ."

"Still, it has to be *someone.*"

"Yes," said Angel Rose with another unhappy sigh, "it has to be *someone*. That money isn't just floating away."

"After the lights go on again and you're all three back on the platform," said Roger, "would any of them have a chance to slip over there to the office?"

Angel Rose shrugged her plump shoulders.

"Yes. There's no getting around that. Any one of them could slip away for a couple of minutes if he wanted to and we'd never be the wiser. So . . . well, to tell the truth, that's what got me to thinking about these kids," she said, shooting a glance at Roger that set him quivering with eagerness.

She sat forward and spread her hands on the table as though she were putting cards there.

"The thing is, we can't just let things go on this way. We've got to know. Now, we'd like to hire a detective, but we don't dare. Remember, before B.J. reformed them, all three of those men were the sort of sinners who could spot a dick — a detective, that is — a mile off. For that matter, so could B.J. He knows the Light but he knows the world, too. Especially the horses. But if he ever found out we brought in a detective to check on his helpers he'd be so hurt it would like to kill him, because he believes we should all have perfect trust among ourselves. *But . . .*"

Once again Angel Rose turned her brilliant blue eyes Roger's way.

"*But*, one thing B.J. does love is to have boys and girls help with his meetings. He loves to have them help get things ready before the meeting, help take the collection, and then help clean up afterwards and — well, just be around. And he's always glad to pay them liberally. Usually by the time the last meeting is over they get so involved they want to give back their pay, but he says no, the laborer is worthy of his hire, and he always makes them keep at least half. So anyway, if I was to ask an old schoolmate's kids to help out, he'd be tickled to death — and the men would think nothing of it, because they're used to it."

Just as Roger had foreseen, his mother immediately began to worry.

"But — what would you want them to do, Rose?"

"Just two things, Enid, neither of them the least bit dangerous. First, count the money. Next, hide where they can watch the office and see if anyone goes near it."

"But what if someone does come near?" asked Mrs. Tearle nervously.

"Well, don't worry, Enid. I wouldn't expect them to try and tackle him!" said Angel Rose with a throaty chuckle. "All they'd do is watch and see who it was. And even if one of our men does come out of the tent and go in there, that won't prove he's guilty. All of us have keys, all of us have a perfect right to go in that office any time we need to, and we've got plenty of excuses for doing it. Don't forget, Pete and Floyd live in there nights. No, we've got to catch the guilty party with the goods, got to catch him redhanded — and the Lord has already helped me to see the way it can be done. I already had a plan, but I didn't have the help I needed — until you folks came along."

Roger wriggled in his chair like a worm on a hook.

"What's your plan?"

"Well. The way I see it is this. Tomorrow night and Friday night I want you kids to count the money. I don't want it to be only Brother Leroy's word and mine that money has been turning up missing. I want it to be someone from outside, and that has to be someone whose word will be believed by everyone, including the law if necessary. Now, when I heard about how you stand with the State Police, Roger, I knew you had been sent to me as that someone. So anyway, after you count the money you go outside and keep watch. And if money keeps turning up missing and if we get a notion as to who might be taking it, then on Saturday night . . ."

Angel Rose paused, and her blue eyes glinted.

"Saturday night," she said, "we'll mark the money!"

The eyes of his family, and Thumbs's as well, turned toward Inspector Tearle. He knew what they were thinking. He was glorying in the same thought himself.

"Roger! How about your ultraviolet lamp?" cried Shirley.

"That's right," he agreed, and tried not to look too smug as he turned to Angel Rose. "I've got just the outfit for that job. I'll get it and show you."

He hurried up to his room, rooted around in his closet, and returned with an odd-looking lamp and a small bottle of liquid. He set the lamp on the table and plugged its cord into an outlet.

"I bought this at an auction when a dance hall over in Burgessville went broke. They used to stamp the back of everybody's hand to keep track of who had paid and to keep out gate-crashers."

Roger opened the bottle. A small brush was attached to the inside of the screw-on cap.

"They put some of this stuff on a stamp pad. See, it's colorless and invisible," he said, brushing a little on the back of his hand. "But under the light —"

He held his hand under the ultraviolet light. The mark showed as a glowing shade of violet.

Angel Rose was delighted.

"That beats the way I had in mind, and it's faster, too. Why, we can mark the edges of a whole batch of bills with that in no time at all! Roger, the Lord knew what He was doing when He sent you to me!"

She turned to Mrs. Tearle.

"What about it, Enid? Would you mind if they helped us out?"

"Well . . ." Mrs. Tearle exchanged an uncertain glance with her husband. "You're sure it wouldn't be dangerous?"

"Dangerous?" Inspector Tearle was quick to reject the suggestion, and very anxious to do so. "What danger could there be, Mom? Why, compared to what went on over at Mrs. Hargrove's place* —"

"Ha! And you know what I had to say about *that*, when I found out what you'd been up to!"

Roger could recall her scolding quite well. But he could also recall her pride in what he had accomplished.

It was only a matter of time before she had to give in.

---

* See *The Case of the Silver Skull*, pp. 100–118.

Four

EVEN THOUGH IT HAD worked to his advantage in this case, age is a problem for a twelve-year-old detective. For example, the question of transportation was a sticking point for a while.

Roger wanted to bike it both ways, of course — he preferred to be strictly on his own — but his mother firmly vetoed the prospect of a four-mile bike ride home at ten o'clock at night.

"We'll drive you over and come get you," she said.

"Nursery school stuff!" cried Inspector Tearle, offended. He was not about to suffer overprotection if he could help it.

"I'll have someone pick you up," said Angel Rose.

"And let everybody in town see one of your campers doing it?" Roger shook his head. "That's going to be a problem, anyway. People who know me are likely to show up at your meetings, and they'll wonder why I'm there —"

"Don't worry about that, everybody around here knows you've always got your nose into anything that's going on," said his father. But Roger stubbornly stuck to his guns, and finally a compromise was reached. They would ride their bikes as far as Mrs. Wimble's cottage on the outskirts of town, leave their bikes in her yard, and be picked up there.

Promptly at seven o'clock, as they waited beside the road near Mrs. Wimble's cottage, a camper appeared with Floyd at the wheel.

"You the kids Angel Rose sent me for? Well, hop in, we ain't got all night," he said, and they joined him briskly in the wide cab of the camper. "I hope you work out better than some of the kids B.J. takes on. Some of 'em are darn poor help."

"We'll do our best," said Roger, as Floyd turned the camper around. Unlike Homer's pale and watery eyes, Floyd's were sharp and shrewd. He gave them a quick, appraising look and made a grumping sound in his throat.

"He says, 'Suffer little children to come unto me,' so they come — and we do the suffering, trying to keep 'em out from underfoot."

The rest of the ride was accomplished in silence. It was obvious that Floyd could have done without them, but at least, Roger decided, the ex-con man did not seem to suspect them of being anything more than potential nuisances.

When they reached the tent, Angel Rose was on the lookout for them and took them in to meet the Reverend Buddy Joe. She was not dressed yet for her appearance on the platform, and neither was he. In work clothes he looked more like the foreman of a construction gang than a preacher.

He seemed as pleased as Angel Rose had said he would be.

"I can't tell you the lift it gives me to have youngsters help with our good work," he boomed. "You're the hope of tomorrow, and we need you. And you'll each and every one of you get fifteen dollars when we finish up here Saturday night, because the laborer is worthy of his hire!"

In many ways B.J. reminded Roger of Mr. Chadburn, their friend at Hessian Run Farm. He was the same sort of short, stout, red-faced little rooster of a man. It would have been easy to find him ridiculous and even dubious, yet something about him led Roger to reserve judgment. Was he merely a crowd-rouser who was making a good thing out of religion or did he really mean the things he said?

"So you two are twins, hey?" he remarked as his large and somewhat protuberant eyes twinkled back and forth between Roger and Shirley. "I'd never have guessed it —

but then, boy and girl twins aren't ever identical, are they?"

"No, sir. And this is our friend Thumbs Thorndyke."

"Thumbs? Where did he ever get a handle like that?"

"It's short for All Thumbs, because that's the way he is," said Shirley, while Thumbs grinned sheepishly. "He's got two left feet, too."

"He's at the awkward age. He's been there for years," said Roger. "If he doesn't stumble over a tent peg, we'll be lucky."

"I haven't fallen over anything for a week!" Thumbs protested.

"Well, just don't drop the collection, sonny," said B.J., winking at him, "though folks are awful good to us and we don't hear anything jangle once in a blue moon."

And then, as quickly as he had winked, his face became solemn and earnest and he stabbed out a finger at them in a familiar platform gesture.

"Don't forget, that's blessed money you're handling — or leastways soon will be. Every bit of it is going to do good in this world. Homer!" he bawled, shifting gears again as Homer came down the aisle carrying a large potted plant intended to decorate a corner of the platform, "here's some youngsters are going to lend a hand."

Homer's watery eyes swam back and forth, taking them in with about as much pleasure as Floyd had shown.

"Okay. Just don't mess with the electrical stuff, is all," he cautioned.

"Homer plays those rheostats as pretty as Brother Leroy plays the organ," said B.J.

"I'll show the kids around," said Angel Rose, "and then I'll turn them over to Brother Leroy to do the leaflets."

She led them to the area behind the tent where the vehicles were parked.

"We're like a regular circus parade when we're on the road," she said. "B.J. and Brother Leroy live in the other campers, and we all drive our own. Floyd drives the office, and Homer drives the van. Once when Homer did some backsliding and fell into the clutches of his old enemy, Pete had to drive the van till Homer sobered up, but that hasn't happened for a long time."

The bus had a single door at the front with a business-like lock on it. Venetian blinds shielded the windows, even the windshield. Inspector Tearle stared at the words that glittered along the side of the bus and felt a familiar skin-crawl of excitement. What light might be spread on dark secrets inside that office before the week was over?

"You all have keys to this, you said?"

"Yes. And like I told you last night, a perfect right to go in and out whenever we want to. So don't jump to any conclusions, no matter who you see — unless it's a stranger, and then you come a-running!"

She took them back to the tent and introduced them to Brother Leroy, who blinded them with a smile that seemed a yard wide and solid ivory. He picked up a stack of leaflets lying on top of the organ and divided them up.

"Here you are, put one on every chair, kids," he said, and assigned them each a section. Around them everybody was busy with something, getting ready for the night's performance. There was an atmosphere of hustle and bustle in the tent which Roger found exhilarating, and Brother Leroy sensed this.

"Holy show biz, I call it," he told them with a grin. "I used to be in show business, wasting my time, going nowhere, before I saw the Light and found out that this was where some real good can be done. Helping folks every night — there's nothing like it! I want to tell you, kids, every one of us here was a sinner before we saw the Light — that's what's so great about it." He dropped his voice confidentially, and his eyes flicked toward the back of the tent where the three helpers were straightening lines of chairs. "Angel Rose told me all about you. I think it's a great idea. You do your best, and we'll clear up this terrible problem we're having. Now, get going with those leaflets!"

Anyone who wants to be a detective must expect to find himself doing things from time to time that go against the grain. For Roger, helping to take up the collection was one of those things. He felt terribly self-conscious as he went up a side aisle shoving his collection bag in front of one row of people after another. For one thing, just as he had expected, there were people present who knew him — Mrs. Hargrove's old gardener Wilfred Humbert and his wife Aggie, for example. But oddly enough, they paid little attention to his presence there. All of them were too busy pressing their offerings between their fingers and praying and listening to the Reverend Buddy Joe.

Roger watched Wilfred's gnarled fingers drop a couple of dollar bills into the bag and Aggie's do the same. He watched and thought about how hard they had to work for what little they had, and he was angry. Until that moment the whole affair of the missing money had been a game to him, an adventure; now, suddenly, he saw it as a contemptible abuse of the simple trust of two old

friends, and he was angry. From that moment on, catching the thief meant something to him personally.

With eight of them working at it the collection was swiftly finished. They gathered in the rear section of the tent, where the three helpers handed their bags to Brother Leroy.

"Come along, kids," said Angel Rose, and led the way out into the dark. Once outside, Brother Leroy handed the bags to her and hurried ahead to unlock the office door.

"See you later," he said, and stayed outside while the rest of them filed inside behind Angel Rose. The poles were awkward to maneuver through the doorway, and of course Thumbs managed to give Roger a whack on the side of his head with the end of his pole.

"Sorry, Roger!"

"Well, watch where you swing that thing, will you?"

"Pull the door shut, Shirley," said Angel Rose. She laid her five bags of money on one of the bunks and told them to put theirs on the other. The bunks were against the wall on each side of a table. On the table sat a large square box covered inside and out with shiny blue quilted cloth. Angel Rose posted herself behind the table, told them to sit on the corners of the bunks, and said, "Now! Let's get busy!"

Five

Each of you take a bag and dump the money on the table and start counting. Count a hundred dollars at a time, throw it in the box, and make a mark on one of those pads," said Angel Rose, pointing to pads and pencils lying on the table.

Emptying out the bags was also an awkward business. The air seemed to be full of poles, and this time Thumbs nearly poked Shirley in the eye.

"Sorry, Shirl! I was just trying to make sure I got everything out of my bag!"

"Okay, Thumbs. Wow! A twenty! I'll start with that," said Shirley, gathering up a handful of bills and beginning to count.

"Don't just take all the big ones!" snapped Roger, trying to keep up with her flying fingers. But Shirley had her first hundred ready before he did.

"There!" She reached up and tossed it into the Blessing Box and made a mark on her pad.

"Forty-one, forty-two — no, three . . . Darn it, these bills stick together," grumbled Thumbs, who was living up to his nickname. Angel Rose suddenly held up one hand nervously.

"What was that?" she whispered, and they all turned in panic toward the door, listening hard.

"Never mind, it couldn't be anyone. Brother Leroy's standing watch," she decided. "But listen, I think if two of you stay in here to count the money and one keeps watch outside it'll be better, especially when Brother Leroy and I have to go back to the tent. Thumbs, why don't you do that?"

Roger kept his face straight, but he was grinning inside, and he knew Shirley was, too. Angel Rose was no dummy; she could see that Thumbs was not cut out for this kind of work. Roger helped her out.

"That's a great idea, and nobody's a better lookout than Thumbs," he said. "He can do an owl hoot that nobody but an Indian would know was anything but an owl hooting!"

"Besides," sighed Thumbs, who was always honest about everything, including himself, "I'm a rotten counter."

"All right, then, slip outside and keep watch," said Angel Rose, giving him a pat on the shoulder, and Thumbs left them.

After that things went along much more smoothly. Even so, it took quite a while to count a hundred dollars when a good deal of it was in ones.

"I've got to go," said Angel Rose presently. "Finish up as soon as you can, and be sure to shut the door behind you. It's got a spring lock."

"I know," said Roger, who always took note of such details.

"And don't forget to bring along your tallies."

"We won't."

"And turn off the lights."

"Okay."

She beamed at them from the door.

"You're doing fine. We'll figure this thing out, you wait and see!" she said, and left them to their work.

It was one thing to count the money with Angel Rose standing there and quite another to sit counting it alone. The atmosphere had changed unpleasantly. It was hard not to jump at every sound that came from outside, and when they spoke, it was in whispers.

"Hurry up, Roger! I'm way ahead of you!"

"Listen, it's not supposed to be a contest," he retorted severely. "Just be sure you're accurate —"

"I am — but I want to get through, too. I'm nervous!"

"Well, you don't have to worry yet," said Roger, seeing in his mind's eye the action over at the tent. Homer would be standing at his control board, busy with his rheostats. Pete and Floyd would be rolling down the side-walls. "We have until the lights go out and then come on again before there's anything to be nervous about, because none of those men can leave the tent till then."

"There could always be a first time. What if Thumbs does hoot?"

"I was thinking about that," Roger admitted. He stood up and dropped to his knees for a look behind the slip-cover that covered the bunk and hung down almost to the floor along its side. "Good! There's plenty of room under here to hide. If Thumbs ever hoots, just drop to the floor and roll out of sight under that bunk."

Feeling a bit more secure, they resumed their counting. Before long they were down to the odd amounts they had left over after counting their last even hundred. Shirley finished up and counted her marks.

"Seven hundred and seventy-six dollars!"

Roger limped in a bad second with $551. By the time he finished and quickly totaled their amounts, Shirley was kneeling on her bunk peeping out between the slats of a blind.

"The lights just went out in the tent! Let's get out of here!"

"No!" Roger was not an amateur magician for nothing. He knew the value of distractions, and how to use them. "We'll leave the instant the lights come on again. That's when the men will all be so busy there won't be a chance of their looking this way."

"Well, that'll be any second, so —"

"Say the word, and I'll open the door."

"Okay — now!"

Even at a distance the sudden organ music and Angel Rose's earsplitting "Hallelujah" made Shirley's warning unnecessary. Roger turned out the lights and pushed open the door. They popped outside like two Mexican jumping beans, and Roger swung the door shut behind them. He was very glad the night was black and moon-less.

They knew Thumbs was hiding behind Homer's van and they had already picked their own spots for the stake-out — Roger behind Angel Rose's camper, Shirley behind the next one. Sprinting off into the darkness, they flung themselves down in the grass where they would be con-cealed but could watch the office door.

Roger mopped his forehead with a hand as clammy as his brow was sweaty and blew out a breath of relief. The worst was over now, and the solution of the case might come at any minute — or if not the solution, at least the beginning of one. If, in the next few minutes, someone paid the office a visit, they might not have conclusive evi-dence, but they would certainly have a good suspect.

Two or three minutes dragged by, and Roger regretted every one of them. There was not much time left before the meeting ended. Inside the tent a final hymn was being sung. Could it be they had drawn a blank? Why was the thief staying away tonight? Was he on to them?

Had they — to use the language of the detective's trade — had they somehow blown their cover? . . .

No!

A shadow was moving. It was moving between the back of the tent and the office. Quickly, and yet without seeming to hurry, it reached the office door. A pause, a click; the door swung open and a small figure slipped inside.

It was all Roger could do to hold back a groan of frustration. Who was it? First he had been sure it was Homer. Then Pete. Then Floyd. He could only hope that Thumbs, who had the best cat's eyes and hearing of them all, had been able to tell.

In a matter of seconds, the door opened again and the

shadow crossed back to the tent, and now Roger was wishing the night had not been so black and moonless after all. Who was it? He still could not tell. He waited for another long minute. He could hear the benediction being pronounced by the Reverend Buddy Joe.

"Psst!"

Roger shot convulsively to his feet.

"Roger?"

"Shirley! Darn you, you scared the life out of me!"

"Well, come on! He's gone!"

"I know! Could you tell who he was?"

"No."

"Neither could I. But I'll bet Thumbs will know."

"I hope so!"

They picked their way across the lot to the van, and Roger whispered,

"Thumbs?"

Their friend materialized silently out of the dark.

"Could you tell who it was?"

"Yes. It was Pete."

Roger's grin all but lit up the darkness.

"Attaboy! Maybe you can't count money," he said, "but what would we do without you?"

The meeting had ended. Standing in the back, they watched the crowd get to their feet and slowly head for the parking lot, all of them seeming to talk at once. By twos and threes they flowed around each side of the platform toward the front entrance, which had been opened wide.

Brother Leroy stayed at the organ, playing "Lead Kindly Light" at a definitely cheerful tempo, smiling and speaking to people as they passed. The Reverend Buddy Joe and Angel Rose had left the scene. A moment earlier the audience had been asked to remain seated until they had gone. He had come up one aisle and she the other, beaming at one and all and saying "Goodnight and God bless you all!" several times as they came. Angel Rose had glanced briefly at Roger with a question in her eyes which he had answered with a nod. She seemed to catch her breath a bit, but walked on and disappeared around the partition at the rear. Later on, when B.J. had given her his tally, she would send for them, and then . . .

When the tent had cleared, when headlights were going on and motors starting and car doors slamming and horns honking out in the parking lot, they reported to Pete, who was in charge of cleanup operations. It was not easy to act naturally in front of the very man who had turned into their prize suspect, but they did their best. Fortunately he was too preoccupied to notice them much. The small man gave them each a large plastic bag and said, "Put all the trash in these, and any lost articles you find, bring 'em to me. Collect the leaflets left on the chairs and give 'em to Brother Leroy."

By now, thought Roger, B.J. was probably out in the office. They had been careful to mix the bills around in

47

the Blessing Box after they finished their count so that it would not look as if it had been touched. Roger pictured the stocky little man, a bit weary now after his workout, scooping bills together and putting them on the table, then settling down to his counting. Did he really bless each and every one of those bills as he counted them? What was really going on out there?

It took quite a while to clean up after the crowd. Religion, it seemed, did not stop people from being litterbugs. There was plenty of litter around and under the chairs, especially leaflets people had managed to drop. The young helpers also came across two shabby wallets, empty, one lipstick, four handkerchiefs, a corncob pipe, a pocket comb, a box of cough drops, and one umbrella, despite the fact that the possibility prediction for rain had been zero. When Shirley found the umbrella, they were almost through. By then they had been working for nearly half an hour.

"Some folks would carry an umbrella to the Sahara," grumbled Pete when Shirley brought it to him. "Tomorrow they'll turn up looking for it. Okay, kids, I guess that's it for tonight."

Brother Leroy, who had been standing behind the last row of seats with a waiting air, came down the aisle toward them. He cast a sardonic eye in Pete's direction as the little man left to add their finds to his lost-and-found collection.

"Quite a switch for old Pete," remarked Brother Leroy. "He *returns* wallets now instead of lifting them. Say, Angel Rose wants to see you before you go," he added, giving Roger a meaningful look. "She's out in her camper."

Roger nodded eagerly. "Okay, we'll go right out."

"You got something?"

"Yes."

Brother Leroy's eyes glittered at the news.

"Okay. You go tell her about it."

Roger checked his watch. B.J. had finished up in less than half an hour. Pretty fast blessing, that would be, and yet with practice it was not unthinkable, and could even be sincere.

When he tapped on the camper door Angel Rose opened it almost immediately, and light framed her in the doorway as dazzlingly as it had that first time, even though she had now changed to a pink dressing gown. She held a slip of paper in her hand.

"Did you see anyone?"

"Yes. Pete."

"He went in?"

"Yes. In and out in a hurry."

Shaking her head slowly, she let out an unhappy sigh.

"Well . . . let's see if we agree. What's your total, Roger?"

"Thirteen hundred and twenty-seven dollars."

49

Angel Rose stared down at him. Then she handed him the slip of paper. Roger unfolded it and read the scrawled figures: twelve hundred and seventeen.

Exactly one hundred and ten dollars short.

"My gosh! Then —"

"Now, wait! He's innocent till proven guilty, and we haven't proved anything yet," she said. "But — well, it looks bad. We'll just have to see what tomorrow brings — and Saturday night."

She looked as if she were ready to burst into tears.

"Thanks a million, kids — and now, go find Floyd and he'll take you back. I just don't feel like talking about this anymore tonight," she said, and closed the door, leaving them in darkness.

Six

WELL, YOU DONE BETTER than some," was the grudging tribute Floyd paid them as he drove them back to East Widmarsh. That was about all he had to say until he let them out, when he added, "See you here same time tomorrow night." So it was a silent trip, since the matters that were on their minds were hardly ones they could discuss in front of Floyd.

When they walked into Mrs. Wimble's driveway to fetch their bikes, the cottage door opened.

"Hi, kids. Just wanted to be sure it was you and not some sneak thieves," she said. "How did it go? Find out anything interesting?"

Roger had explained that they were "looking into something" over at the revival meetings and had asked her not to say anything about it to anybody. One consideration that had led him to suggest her cottage as a meeting place was that he knew she could be trusted not to talk. He had reason to know. They were good friends, especially since the affair at Mrs. Hargrove's big place across the road.

"Well, yes, it was an interesting evening," he said now, and Mrs. Wimble laughed.

"All right, Roger, I won't pry — but I want to hear all about it after you're through! Oh, and by the way, I'd like an extra dozen Large on Saturday, I'm having company."

"Yes, ma'am. I'll write it down as soon as we get home."

It was Roger the Egg Baron who was talking now. He and Shirley and Thumbs sold Mr. Chadburn's eggs all over East Widmarsh, traveling a regular route each morning on their well-laden bicycles. The profits were helping to build their college funds.

Bidding Mrs. Wimble goodnight, they pedaled swiftly homeward along the quiet roads, enjoying the cool air, but now it was Inspector Tearle who was back in the saddle, pondering the events of the evening. When they reached the village square in the center of town, he called for a halt.

"Let's have a talk before we get home and have to start telling Mom and Dad about it," he said. "A lot of things are bothering me."

They leaned their bikes against a park bench and sat down cross-legged on the grass. The square was deserted, silent, and peaceful. In that tranquil place it was hard to believe that only four miles away there was an atmosphere seething with undercurrents and someone helping himself to a revival meeting's collection money.

"Well, what do we know?" Inspector Tearle began abruptly. "We know how much money we counted, and we know how much B.J. reported, and we know the amounts aren't the same. We know Pete is the only person who went into the office before B.J. did. But Angel Rose says he's innocent till proven guilty, and she's right. And if he happens to be innocent, then that only leaves one other possibility."

"You mean, B.J.?"

"Yes."

"But why would he take the money? I mean, he's the boss, he can do what he likes. He could just give himself a bigger salary if he wanted to."

"Yes, but he wants people to think he takes only a small salary. And don't forget, he doesn't know someone else is counting the money before he does. As long as he thinks he's the only one who's counting it, why, he could report any old amount he pleased — within reason, of course — and figure no one would notice any difference."

"Yes, but Angel Rose and Brother Leroy noticed it."

"Well, that's the way people usually get caught — by underestimating other people."

"But . . . do you think B.J. would do that?" asked Thumbs, shocked and troubled by the idea.

"Do you?" countered Roger.

Thumbs frowned over this for a moment.

"N-no, I think he's probably okay," he finally declared without too much certainty.

"I hope you're right. But as Angel Rose said, it has to be *someone*. That money isn't just floating away. And we've only got two someones to choose from."

"Well," said Shirley, "maybe we'll just have to wait till Saturday night to know for sure."

"Maybe," said Inspector Tearle, "but maybe we can wrap it up *before* then. I've got an idea . . ."

He enjoyed the predictable stir this made among his assistants.

"What?" asked Shirley.

"What are you going to do?" asked Thumbs.

"Well, we won't tell anybody about this beforehand, not even Angel Rose, because she might decide it was dangerous," said Roger, "but here's what I thought I would do . . ."

When they reached the fairgrounds the next evening they reported to Pete. Shirley and Thumbs went straight to work, but Roger said, "My mother gave me a message for Angel Rose. I'll be right back," and went on out to her camper.

He did have a message for her, but more than that he was anxious to hear what her thoughts were by now.

"Come in, Roger."

"Thanks. Mom told me to ask you to come over again tonight, if you can."

"Well, you thank her, Roger, but I don't think I'd better tonight," said Angel Rose. "Maybe tomorrow night, after . . . after . . ."

"Okay," said Roger, and went on to more pressing matters. "Well, ma'am, what do you think?"

She sat down on her bed-sofa and sighed gustily.

"Oh, I don't know what to think. I could hardly sleep last night." She shook her head sadly. "I can tell you one thing, if it *is* Pete we'll have a time with him. I can hear him now. He'll say he was framed, he'll say one of the others had a grudge against him and planted the money on him. I just hope that *somehow* it isn't him, that's all."

"Well, we'll just have to see," said Roger, and fought down a quiver of excitement at the thought of his secret plan. If all went well, they might not have to wonder much longer. "So tonight we do the same as last night?"

"Yes. Count the money, then watch to see if Pete goes in again. And then tomorrow night . . ."

Roger left her and hurried back to the tent.

Try as he might, Roger could not challenge his sister's nimble fingers. Once again she had a hundred in the box and was marking down her tally before he did.

"Say, did I see a fifty in that pile?" asked Angel Rose, peering down at the money on the table in front of them.

"A fifty! Wow-ee!" cried Shirley, and they both pawed through the pile, but failed to uncover any such bonanza.

"Darn! Wishful thinking, I guess, but I sure thought I saw one," said Angel Rose. "It's quite an event when a fifty turns up — though for that matter, B.J.'s reported hundred-dollar bills twice in the collection, but those were on pretty special nights."

The collection looked about the same as the one the night before. They even made a small bet on how close it would be — after Angel Rose had left, of course. She watched while they got started, but by now her confidence in them was such that she left sooner than she had the night before.

Practice makes perfect, or at least something much closer to it. Both of them were faster and they finished with time to spare. Roger added up their results, announced a total of $1439, and said, "Okay, you win the doughnut," referring to a lone survivor they both knew about in the breadbox at home. Shirley's guess had been closer. "Now, get ready to take off."

"The lights haven't gone off yet," she said, checking through the slats of the blind. "Listen, Roger, why can't I —"

"No! Twice as much chance of making a noise —"

"Oh, all right — but you have all the fun!"

"It won't be much fun if anything goes wrong," he reminded her grimly, "so stop arguing."

"The lights went out!" she announced.

"Okay," said Roger a bit breathlessly — his heart was beginning to beat faster despite his best efforts to remain calm. He went to the door. "When I open up, get moving! I'll pull it shut."

The organ and Angel Rose both sounded their notes. Roger snapped off the light and opened the door. Shirley leaped into the darkness. Roger pulled the door shut.

Feeling his way back to one of the bunks, he dropped to the floor, lifted the edge of the slipcover, and wriggled underneath. He made sure the cloth was hanging straight, then settled himself into the most comfortable position he could find.

It was not overly comfortable.

Seven

INSPECTOR TEARLE HAD NEVER slept in an upper berth on a train, but he imagined it would seem much like his present surroundings, though probably softer and not quite as dusty.

Struggling to get his hand in his pocket, he managed to pull out his handkerchief and give his nose a good blow. He was not anxious to find himself fighting a sneeze at a crucial moment, if a crucial moment presented itself.

He had spent some long sessions in tight quarters on other occasions, but none quite as constricting as his present one. There was precious little vertical space under his bunk, not nearly as much as there had seemed to be when he had optimistically surveyed his hiding place from above. Once again he reminded himself that the detective business was bound to have its trying moments. His body seemed to be all bones, and every bone was finding something to make itself uncomfortable against.

At the same time, of course, he was listening hard, half afraid of what he would hear and half afraid he would not hear anything. Dimly, after a while, the music of the final hymn reached his ears and his nerve began to falter. What if he lingered too long and failed to leave before B.J. came out? He scringed at the thought. If something didn't happen very soon, he would have to give up and leave in a hurry. If —

"Wh-o-o-o-o!"

Somewhere out in the darkness an owl hooted, an owl that only an Indian would have known was not an owl hooting. Roger's head jerked up so sharply he gave it a good bump on the bottom of the bunk. And he didn't even dare rub it. He simply froze and waited.

A key slid into the lock. The door opened and closed, and someone was breathing in the darkness of the office. Not Roger, to be sure — he was holding his breath and listening as he had never listened before.

Light!

A band of light glowed between the floor and the edge of the slipcover as the lights were switched on. Roger sucked his breath in, despite himself. Feet passed him, inches away. They paused, shuffled, turned back, and passed again, stepping almost noiselessly.

And suddenly, with gritty edges as sharp as knives, dust tickled his nostrils.

He grabbed his nose and pinched it together hard. Was the movement fatal? Had his elbow brushed against the slipcover? The feet stopped. An eternity passed while Roger suffered. Then the soft rasp of the footsteps began again. The lights clicked off; the door opened and quietly closed.

Somehow he managed to count fairly slowly to twenty-two before, explosively, he sneezed.

The benediction was being pronounced by the Reverend Buddy Joe in the big tent when Roger all but dived out of the office, so relieved was he to be clear of it. His satisfaction was, however, purely physical. His mind was disturbed by what he considered to be an inexplicable failure. All the misery he had endured in there had been for nothing. Instead of being closer to the solution of the case, he was utterly baffled.

Two figures converged on him out of the darkness, eager for news. They barely kept their voices low.

"Well?"

"Thumbs, was it Pete again?"

"Sure, Roger. Did he —"

"No!" Roger spoke almost peevishly. "I didn't hear one thing!"

"What?"

"Not a single bill rustled!"

"That's crazy!" said Shirley. "Thumbs should have been in there, with his good hearing."

"Listen, maybe I don't have ears as keen as his, but I don't have to use an ear trumpet, either!" snapped Roger. "I tell you, I didn't hear a rustle! And don't tell me anybody, even an ex-pickpocket, could lift a hundred dollars' worth of bills out of that box without making a sound! But come on, we haven't got time to talk about it now, we've got to show up in there!"

They slipped inside and were again standing behind the last row of chairs when B.J. and Angel Rose came up the aisles. Again she glanced their way, and again Roger nodded. She flowed on up the aisle in her long white robe and disappeared.

"No sense in telling her what I did," he muttered with a depressing guilty feeling, "especially when there's nothing to tell. Maybe I'll tell her later, but for now I want to think about it. I just can't understand . . ."

Their cleanup operations were much the same as the

night before, the only variation being in the lost articles they came across. This time there was only one wallet, a fat, bulging one. The owner showed up, perspiring freely, before they had even finished, and was very glad to see it again. Besides the wallet there were a set of keys, a pocket mirror, a nail clipper, an empty coin purse, two lipsticks, three handkerchiefs, a pocket calendar advertising a Burgessville bank — and no umbrellas.

"No umbrellas?" said Pete, when they had finished up. "Hey, Floyd, I got to mark this day down in my calendar, it's a red-letter day — no umbrellas!"

He turned back to his junior staff and remarked almost genially, "Just like I told you he would, some old gent turned up this morning looking for that umbrella you found last night. And hey, Floyd, guess what he was? A justice of the peace!"

Floyd snickered.

"Well, the rain falls on the just and the unjust, so why not on the justice of the peace, too?"

"You better watch that stuff, or B.J. will be giving you what-for again," Pete warned, but Floyd only chuckled and said, "I'll be outside when you're ready to go, kids."

"That Floyd, he's always making puns and jokes on the Scriptures, and B.J., he don't like it," he explained. "He gets on Floyd about it every so often."

Roger grinned.

"When Floyd picked us up last night, he said, 'B.J.

says, "Suffer little children to come unto me" — and we do the suffering.' "

Pete burst into genuine laughter and slapped Roger on the shoulder.

"That son-of-a-gun! I oughtn't to laugh, but that's pretty good!"

Slapping him on the shoulder — this man whose feet, half an hour ago, had been six inches from Roger's nose in the dark of the office! And yet, as they left Pete and went up the aisle toward Brother Leroy, who once again happened to be there, all Roger could find to mutter to Shirley and Thumbs was, "You know, it's hard not to like those old guys."

And was Pete really the villain of the piece after all, for that matter? Roger was no longer sure, if he ever had been.

"She's ready to see you," murmured Brother Leroy as they joined him. "Did it go the same as last night?"

"Yes."

He whistled mournfully and turned away. They went outside and waved to Floyd, who was waiting at the wheel of Brother Leroy's camper.

"We'll just be a minute," Roger called. "We want to say goodnight to Angel Rose."

Floyd waved a casual hand.

"Take your time," he said. He was becoming almost tolerant.

Angel Rose listened to their total of $1439 and handed them B.J.'s slip. It read: $1329.

Again, exactly $110 short.

Inspector Tearle kept his poker face as he looked at the slip, but his last hope for a quick solution to the case had gone a-glimmering.

"And you saw Pete go in again?"

"Yes."

Angel Rose's head drooped, sending the golden ring-lets tumbling down the front of her pink dressing gown. The strain and anxiety in her face made it appear almost drawn.

"Well, it really does look bad. But . . ."

Her head came up, and her face glowed.

"Anyway, twenty-four hours from now it will all be over!"

"Sure," said Roger, but he wondered if she was right.

Eight

ONCE AGAIN INSPECTOR TEARLE ordered a halt at the village square, and again it proved a good place to have a talk before going home. One or two cars went by, driven by people they knew. Constable Stubbert, East Widmarsh's only law officer, took a turn around the square in the village's only prowl car, but he merely waved and kept going. There had been a time when he would have scowled at the very sight of Inspector Tearle. Not long ago it had been his custom to refer to Roger as the nosiest kid in town; not long ago he had taken a dim view of twelve-year-old sleuths; but now, more than ever, since the Hargrove affair, they were on cordial terms.

First Roger described in detail exactly what had taken place in the office. More important, of course, was what had *not* taken place.

"I tell you, I never heard so much as a suspicion of a

rustle," he insisted. "I'd swear he never touched those bills!"

"But if he wasn't after the money, then why did he come out there?" asked Shirley. "What else could he be after?"

"Yes, and why does he come out every night, then?" added Thumbs.

"We don't know that he does come out *every* night," Roger pointed out in a nitpicking manner. In conferences such as this one, whenever they were trying to work out a puzzle that had him baffled, he tended to be cranky and impatient and to scoff at their ideas. But they were used to him and didn't let it bother them.

"Well, two nights in a row, anyway," said Thumbs mildly.

"Maybe he *is* after something else," said Shirley. "Maybe it's something perfectly all right, something he always wants right after the meeting."

"Like what?"

"Well . . . his cigarettes, maybe."

"Huh! Why wouldn't he have them in his pocket all the time?"

"Well . . . maybe he doesn't want to tempt himself with them till the meeting's over," said Shirley, trying hard to build up a case for her idea, now that it had occurred to her. "I know he does smoke, I saw him outside the tent when we got here tonight."

Roger snorted, and proceeded to demolish her theory.

"All right, let's say that female intuition has done it again and you're right, he came out to get his cigarettes. Then how come I didn't hear the pack crackle when he picked it up? Are you going to tell me anybody is going to pick up a pack of butts without making a sound? I don't say he couldn't — but why would he bother?"

"Maybe it was something else that wouldn't make any noise," said Thumbs.

"Yes, but what?" demanded Roger. "What, if anything? Except for that money, I can't think of anything that would make a man come out there night after night —"

"Wait a minute!" Shirley's face lighted up at the arrival of another idea. "Maybe *he's* checking up on something!"

Inspector Tearle proved he could be gracious about his assistants' ideas when they had unexpected merit. "Now, that's a thought!" he admitted slowly. His gaze, as he stared at his sister, was half-admiring and half-annoyed. "It leaves things in a worse muddle than ever, but it *is* a thought!"

Shirley was pleased with herself, so pleased that she made an effort to be gracious, too. She accepted his complaint.

"It's a muddle, all right," she admitted. "What *could* he be checking up on?"

"Could there be a switch or something that has to be turned on or off every night after the lights come back on in the tent?" suggested Thumbs.

"No. Angel Rose would know about anything like that," Roger pointed out. "Oh, I give up! I don't know *what* it could be — but I do know one thing, he didn't scoop a hundred and ten bucks' worth of bills out of that box without my hearing it. Do you realize it was the same exact amount both nights, a hundred and ten? Why, he'd have to stop and count it out if he was going to take exactly that much! So he didn't take it, and that means we're down to one possibility."

They eyed each other silently for a moment, and then Shirley made the unnecessary identification.

"B.J."

"I don't see any way around it. He's skimming off a little something extra for himself."

"Income tax," said Thumbs suddenly, and now it was he who drew an accolade from Inspector Tearle.

"You're right! Why didn't I think of that? That way he could build himself up a nice bankroll without having to pay taxes on it!"

"Maybe he's sending it to a Swiss bank account," said Thumbs, enjoying the limelight.

"Why not? He wouldn't be the first one!"

For a moment Roger was elated. He felt they had made a real breakthrough. But then his face fell as he saw the matter in another light.

"Oh, boy. Tomorrow night Angel Rose is going to get them all out there in the office after B.J.'s counted the money, and she's going to ask them to produce any money they have on them. She'll tell them about the shortages, and say that the only way they can all be cleared is by showing that they didn't take any of the money. And then everybody's money, one batch at a time, will go under the lamp . . ."

Shirley and Thumbs knew all this, of course, but Roger was not saying it for their benefit. He was merely talking as he built up the scene in his mind, previewing what would happen.

"And then, if it turns out to be *B.J.* who has the marked money, Angel Rose is just going to die," Roger went on gloomily. "Do you realize what it's going to mean to her, and to Brother Leroy — to all of them, for that matter? It'll be the end of their jobs, the end of everything — because how can they go on if they know the boss is a thieving hypocrite?"

There was a long silence while they considered the unhappy situation that was suddenly confronting them. It was Roger who finally broke the silence with a bitter comment.

"I'll tell you the truth," he said. "I wish we'd never gotten involved in this one!"

But involved they were, and there was nothing to do but follow the case through to its dismal conclusion.

Roger was so dissatisfied with himself and so preoccupied that he forgot to bring in Mrs. Wimble's extra dozen Large the next morning and had to go back out to his bike for them.

"You look off your feed, Roger," she told him. "Troubles?"

"Well, yes."

"Is it that business you're looking into over at the revival?"

"Yes."

"I can't wait to hear all about it."

"You won't have to wait long now," he assured her grimly.

"I suppose not. Tonight's the last night, isn't it?"

"Yes, ma'am."

The last night was right.

One reason Roger was dissatisfied with himself was that he felt he had muffed an important detail of operational procedures.

"Why didn't I give Angel Rose the lamp and the bottle of liquid to take back with her the night she was at our house?" he complained to his assistants during a stop on their egg route. "Now what am I doing to do? I don't like to turn up carrying a box under my arm tonight. Floyd's sure to be curious."

"Well, why don't you say it's something Mom is sending to Angel Rose?" suggested Shirley.

"I suppose I can do that, but I don't like having to make up a story about it when I could just as easily have gotten it over there without any problem," grumbled Roger. "I should have looked ahead. I think I'm losing my grip!"

He felt very unprofessional and didn't like it.

Fortunately Fate tired of kicking him around at that point and took pity on him. Roger's father announced he was going to drive over to Burgessville on an errand after lunch, and his mother asked if he would stop by and urge Angel Rose to pay them a farewell visit after the final meeting that evening.

"Say! Can I go with you, Dad?" asked Roger. "That way I can give her the marking stuff and the lamp without anyone knowing about it! In fact, *you* can even hand her the package, and they'll just think it's something from you and Mom."

"You'd think they were all watching your every move over there, Roger," said Mr. Tearle.

"You never know," he retorted darkly. "You can't be too careful."

"Well, okay, but I'll probably be a couple of hours in Burgessville, so if you don't want to come along I'll give her the stuff for you."

"No, I'd like to come. I can always find things to do in Burgessville, or maybe I'll just stay at the tent and see if I can help with anything there, and you can pick me up on the way back."

"Suit yourself," said Mr. Tearle. "I'm always ready to do anything to help in the fight against crime."

All was not perfect, but at least matters had improved in the world of Inspector Tearle.

Nine

Except to shirley and Thumbs, Roger had made no mention of his private investigations in the office the night before. He did not want to be suddenly pulled off the case, which was what might have happened if a certain close relative heard he had been up to any such shenanigans. There were times when he greatly envied adult detectives, who had only Commissioners or Bureau Chiefs to worry about in the way of superiors.

"Don't let anything slip about how I hid in the office," he had cautioned Shirley before they reached home. "We'll just say we counted the money again and it was short again — and that's all we'll tell them for now."

"Well, of course!" Shirley had agreed. "Gee, would Mom ever spiral!"

Thus, as they drove to the fairgrounds, Mr. Tearle had no idea his son's suspicions had shifted to someone other than Pete.

"Well, I'll be interested to hear what comes of this business tonight," he told Roger. "If Pete is the guilty party, and it sure looks as if he is, then poor old B.J. is really in for a shock. One of his flock has backslid. I wonder what he'll do about it?"

"So do I," said Roger. "What do you think of him anyway, Dad?"

"B.J.? One heck of a showman!"

"But do you think he's a phony?"

This time Mr. Tearle's reply was not as prompt. He hesitated.

"We-l-l, who am I to judge a man I know so little about? Judge not that ye be not judged, as the Reverend Buddy Joe himself would no doubt say. Anyway, I can't see where he's doing any real harm, and he might be doing some good. In fact, anybody who sends people home feeling better does *some* good, and he certainly seems to accomplish that much. And then I like the fact he doesn't pretend to pass any miracles — doesn't call any poor cripples up in front of everybody and tell them to throw away their crutches or leg braces and walk, or anything like that."

They had reached the fairgrounds. Mr. Tearle swung off the road into the parking lot.

"Some of the faith healers do that, you know," he continued, "and I've read that some people *do* get up and walk — but I've also read that a week later a good many of them have done themselves so much harm without

75

their wheelchairs or crutches or leg braces that they're worse off than ever. So I'm glad he just sticks to blessing their money and praying. Do you think he actually does bless those bills one by one?"

"He could, if he blesses fast," conceded Roger.

"If I know you, you probably held a stopwatch on him," said Mr. Tearle, and laughed when Roger admitted he had checked how much time B.J. spent alone in the office. He stopped the car and turned off the engine.

"So he blesses them and counts them," he said sardonically. "A nice combination of the spiritual and the practical. Maybe that sums him up. And if I am not mistaken, my dear Watson, here comes our man now," he added in imitation of their mutual hero, Sherlock Holmes. The Reverend Buddy Joe, in his work clothes, had appeared at the entrance to the tent, and now he was walking toward them with his customary energy. Mr. Tearle got out of the car.

"Good afternoon, Mr. Billings. I'm Roger's and Shirley's father."

"Well, I'm glad to meet you," said B.J., pumping his hand. "You've got a fine boy there — and a fine daughter."

"Thank you. We just stopped by on our way to town to see Angel Rose for a minute —"

"You're going into Burgessville?"

"Yes."

"Good! I was hoping you might be, and that maybe I could catch a ride with you."

"Why, of course. I won't be coming back for a couple of hours, but —"

"That's all right, Floyd can come in to pick me up. I'll go speak to him about it and be right back."

"Is Angel Rose around?"

"I just left her in the office."

"Then we'll go out there and be back in just a minute, too. Roger, bring that package, will you?" said Mr. Tearle, and they walked back toward the tent with B.J., parting when he went inside and they continued on around a corner of the tent.

"Smooth. Very smooth, Dad," murmured Roger when he was sure they were out of earshot. "If you ever want to get into detective work, there's a place for you on my staff."

"Thank you, Inspector, I'll think about it."

Mr. Tearle knocked on the office door. Angel Rose opened it and beamed out at them.

"Well, this is a nice surprise! Come in!"

They went inside and explained their errand.

"Good thinking, Roger," she said. "We'll just get this stuff tucked away safely right now."

A built-in cabinet stood against the wall on one side of the office. She unlocked one of its drawers.

"I usually keep the accounting books here, but I've got them over in my camper right now, so there's room here," she said, putting Roger's box inside. She closed the drawer, locked it, and handed him the key. "You hang onto this till tonight — I don't have any pockets in my robe."

"Okay," said Roger, pleased to be in charge, and carefully put the key in the pocket of his chinos.

The invitation to come to their house again was issued and accepted. Then they told her they were about to give B.J. a ride into town. She smiled.

"He's funny about that. When he goes into town anywhere, he likes to slip around unnoticed — incognito, I guess you could call it. If he drove into town in his camper, people would spot him right away, so that's why he likes to hitch a ride."

"I'd think they'd spot him anyhow," said Roger, but she shook her head.

"You wait. You'll see. He'll put on dark glasses, and — well, he'll look like just anybody."

"That's very interesting. Well, I won't keep him waiting any longer," said Mr. Tearle, and he turned to leave. "You coming, Roger?"

"Yes, I think I'll go with you," said Roger, whose plans had changed abruptly. What was B.J. going into town for? Maybe if he went along he would learn something significant. They said good-bye to Angel Rose and returned to the car, intrigued by the new side of B.J. that had been revealed.

And sitting in the car wearing dark glasses they saw a man whom it would indeed have been hard to pick out of a crowd. He had allowed his face to relax and sag, he had drained out of it all that special vitality that set it apart, and he was almost unrecognizable. As Roger and his father approached the car, they could not help exchanging an astonished glance.

"Well, I'll tell you one thing about him," Mr. Tearle muttered, "the man is a consummate actor."

During the short ride into Burgessville they passed the time in polite conversation.

"I'll be obliged if you'll let me off at the next corner," said B.J. as they neared the center of town.

"I'll get out there, too, Dad. I want to go into the record shop," said Roger from the back seat.

"Okay, Roger. Meet me in front of the Cosgrove Building in two hours' time, and don't get into any trouble. And don't buy any records you know I can't stand."

"Gee, Dad, they stopped putting out the kind *you* can stand *years* ago!"

"Get out of here, you fresh kid!" said Mr. Tearle, and B.J. chuckled tolerantly.

When they had gotten out on the corner, Roger said good-bye to B.J. and entered the record shop.

And from that moment on, B.J. was under surveillance.

Standing in front of a rack of records, pretending to look them over, Inspector Tearle watched his man, and he was interested to see that B.J. stepped into an outdoor telephone booth and made a brief call.

When B.J. came out and started walking down the street, Roger left the record shop and drifted along behind.

The trail became more and more interesting because it led to a part of town that was far from the best, the old part of the business district down by the railroad tracks. Burgessville, an old industrial town with a population of 55,000, was the county seat and quite a different place from the village of East Widmarsh.

B.J. was not walking fast. Roger was able to stay well behind without having to worry about losing him, and there were enough people on the streets, even down there, to keep him from being conspicuous.

After a while B.J. came to a shabby café. In front of its painted window lounged a man, lantern-jawed and beetle-browed. B.J. stopped; so did Roger, taking his stand in front of the first store window that offered anything to look at. It contained a dusty display of plumbing fixtures, but it would have to do. Out of the corner of his eye he kept watch on the men down the street.

B.J. handed the other man an envelope, exchanged a few words with him, nodded, and walked around the cor-

ner. The man put the envelope in his pocket and started up the street — in Roger's direction.

It was a moment of decision — Buddy Joe or Lantern Jaw, B.J. or L.J.? — but it did not take Roger long to decide. He had a new man to follow now.

Trying to look as if he were fascinated by a large pink washbowl on chromium legs, he stared into the window and listened for footsteps to approach and pass. The temptation to glance at the man was, of course, the very thing he had to guard against the most. He was successful, but the hairs on the back of his neck bristled when he seemed to feel the man's glance on him as he passed. He kept his gaze riveted on the pink washbowl.

Only when the lantern-jawed man had gone well up the street did Inspector Tearle turn away as casually as he could and begin to stroll, as casually as he could, up the street behind him.

Ten

THE INSTANT INSPECTOR TEARLE saw the Reverend Buddy Joe hand an envelope to a thug who looked as if he might have a police record as long as his arm — and his arms were as long as an ape's — a theory sprang into his mind that was brilliantly complete in every detail.

He was remembering what Angel Rose had said about B.J.'s past, how he knew the world, "especially the horses." Was B.J. himself doing some serious backsliding? Did that envelope contain money? Was Lantern Jaw a bookie, or a bookie's runner, and had B.J. placed a bet with him?

In his extensive reading on the subject of crime, Inspector Tearle had made quite a study of these matters.

At any rate, his course was now clear. Follow L.J. and see where he went. Note the address. Then get in touch with Constable Stubbert, or friends in the State Police if necessary, and find out if that address had anything to do with local gambling interests. Probably he would have to go no further than Constable Stubbert. Whatever his other limitations as a police officer might be, the constable was a *Who's Who* of local criminals and their hangouts, especially in Burgessville, since he had once been a member of the Burgessville police force.

Wherever he was going, L.J. did not seem in any hurry to get there. Like Inspector Tearle himself, he paused now and then to glance in a shop window. But finally, after several blocks had been put behind them, he turned into an alley. Roger's pulse quickened and so did his step. Now they were getting somewhere. Wherever he was going, L.J. must be nearly there.

At the same time, an alley presented problems. He could not simply follow the man into it without becoming dangerously conspicuous. And of course it might be that L.J. was merely cutting through the alley to the next street. Or suppose he stopped for some reason close to the head of the alley? Roger did not want to find himself bumping into L.J. as he rounded the corner.

His best course of action, then, would be to stroll casually ahead, checking the alley out of the corner of his eye to find out what had become of his quarry before making his own move.

Bracing himself, Roger walked forward and shot what he fondly hoped was a veiled glance sideways into the alley.

It was empty.

He crossed the open space without pausing, but then stopped and peeped around the corner for another look. He was pleased with the turn of events. Even if L.J. had broken into a mad run he could hardly have reached the other end of the alley in so short a time. Therefore, he must have gone into one of the buildings that lined the alley.

Now all Roger had to do was check out the location of doorways along the alley and — once he had noted the names of the four streets bounding the block the alley was in — he would have all the information he needed.

To be sure, the business of turning into that narrow alley and walking through it did cause a few prickles to dance along his spine. Blank brick walls closed in around him, towering high enough to block out sunlight and create an almost twilight gloom. He found himself walking as quietly as he could, and rather quickly.

But then he slowed, because ahead of him a door had appeared on his right, a solid steel door that had been painted green sometime in the distant past. Faded lettering suggested that the Hy-Tone Produce Company occupied the premises.

A few yards up ahead on the left was another doorway, a deeper one that looked as if it might be a passageway, but Roger paused for a good look at the Hy-Tone Produce Company's door before going on.

And since he was facing the door, the man who sprang out of the doorway behind him took him completely by surprise.

Before he knew what was happening a large hand was over his mouth, the door was wrenched open, and with an arm twisted painfully behind his back he was shoved inside and sent stumbling up a steep flight of stairs.

At the top of the stairs he was hustled through another doorway into a bare, grimy office where a surprisingly well dressed man was standing behind a desk. He had probably been sitting behind it when the racket coming up the stairs had brought him to his feet.

The well-dressed man stared at Roger with cold blue

eyes. L.J. no longer had his hand over Roger's mouth, but that made no difference, because Roger was too scared to utter a sound anyway.

"Well, well. And what do we have here, Whitney?" the man asked in a steely voice.

Whitney! Even in that moment of terror Roger was struck by the incongruous name. At the very least, a thug like L.J. should have been called Buggsy, or Big Looey, but certainly not Whitney!

"I don't know what he's up to, boss, but this kid was tailing me. After I met a certain party he tailed me back here."

"A *kid* tailed you?" The boss glanced sharply at Roger. "Is that true?"

There was no point in denying it. Instead, Roger blurted out a question.

"How did you know?" he asked Whitney.

It happened to be a good move on his part. It gave Whitney a chance to exercise his vanity.

"Listen, *nobody* can tail me without I know it! But you made it easy," he said. He turned to the boss. "First I come up the street and here's this kid looking real hard into a window where there's nothing but a couple of washbowls and a toilet to look at. That strikes me right away. So I keep going, and check him a couple of times, and sure enough here he comes. And by then I remember where it is I seen him before. He's the kid that his picture was in the paper, the one that helped catch some punks over in East Widmarsh!" he finished triumphantly.

His triumph was short-lived. Clouds gathered on the boss's brow. He shot another frightening glance at Roger.

"Is that true?"

Roger nodded, that being about as much as he could manage just then. The boss's mouth became a hard thin line. He moved toward Whitney in a way that made the thug cringe against the wall.

"Whitney, I ought to stamp on your corn again —"

"No, boss, don't do that!"

"You nitwit! If you could read, instead of just looking at the pictures, you'd have read the whole story about this kid and you'd know he stands in with Dougherty and the State Police like — like — Well, if you wanted to bring Dougherty down on us with both of his big flat feet you couldn't have picked a better kid to push around!"

Whitney licked his lips pathetically.

"But, gee, boss, he was *tailing* me . . ."

"Oh, shut up!"

Even if he had been as dumb as Whitney, Inspector Tearle could hardly have failed to realize that his position was improving by leaps and bounds. He took a deep breath — his first in quite a while — and felt vital energies flooding back into his skinny, quivering frame.

"What's all this about, anyway?" he asked in a voice that cracked only slightly around the edges.

"You tell me," countered the boss.

Roger had the feeling that a strict adherence to facts might continue to be to his advantage, so he answered frankly.

"Well, it's B.J. I'm interested in."

"Why?"

"I wanted to know why he gave something to Whitney, and where Whitney went with whatever B.J. gave him."

"Why?"

"Because I wanted to know what B.J. was doing."

It was a lame answer, but it brought a response that surprised him. Instead of looking angrier, the boss's face suddenly cleared. He threw his head back and laughed.

"Oh, boy. That's good." But immediately he became serious again and stared hard at Roger. "But why did you want to know?"

It was a hard question to field. Too many facts now might be a mistake. Roger thought for a moment, then came up with what seemed like a good compromise.

"Because if he is doing something like playing the horses, it's got to stop," he said.

The boss blinked at that.

"What are you, some kind of junior religious nut?"

"No, but I — I've been asked to find out."

The boss rolled his eyes toward Whitney.

"What's this country coming to? When they start using *kids*, even . . ."

But then he turned back to Roger and his face relaxed again.

"What's your name?"

"Roger."

"Okay, Roger. Mine's Art." He gestured toward a chair beside his desk. "Sit down," he said, and sat down behind the desk.

Roger slid onto the chair, glad to take his weight off his trembling legs. Art leaned forward.

"Now, Roger, I'm going to level with you. You must know something about B.J. or you wouldn't be talking about the horses, but there's a lot you don't know. First of all, he started life as a day laborer and wound up owning his own construction company when he was still a young guy."

Roger thought about the work clothes B.J. wore when he wasn't conducting a meeting and understood now why they seemed so natural on him.

"And in those days," Art went on, "he spent most of what he made on the horses. Every bookie in the country knew him. But then he got religion. And since then — I'd lay any odds on it — he's never put a penny on the nose of a nag again. What you saw him give Whitney here was some money, but it wasn't for a bet."

Art leaned back and shook his head.

"You know, he's quite a guy. His pitch now is helping sinners, as he calls it, and he really believes it. He's got this idea he shouldn't let a day pass but what he helps a sinner personally somewhere — personally but *secretly*. That's one of his Bible ideas. Well, he's *got* to keep it secret, for that matter, because if the word ever got around that he gave handouts to individuals he'd have every down-and-outer in the country on his doorstep. But it's more than that. According to him, the Bible says people ought to do charity in secret, so that's what he does. And all us guys who knew him when, he uses us now to get the money to these people without their knowing where it came from — and how are you going to turn down a man when he comes to you with a proposition like that?"

Art sighed almost regretfully.

"There's something about him . . . well, he makes you do it his way. So now, there's this woman here in town that's at the end of her rope — never mind how she got there, but she's a mess — and I've got to give her this money and see that she goes back home to her family, where she'll have a chance. Now, that's the whole story, and if you ever let it out I'll see to it you wish you hadn't, in spite of Dougherty and every other cop in the country!"

Roger's face made it plain that Art didn't have anything to worry about.

"I won't. I-I'm glad to know it's that way," he said.

Art took a hard look at him and believed him.

"Okay. Now beat it. And from now on, try to go straight. Don't go tailing honest citizens around the streets," he said with only the merest twitch of the lips spoiling his deadpan expression.

"Okay," said Roger, and went to the door. But then he could not resist looking back and asking the honest citizen a question.

"Is your name really Whitney?"

Whitney scowled, and his eyes went this way and that.

"That's what the boss calls me," he mumbled.

"Don't let him kid you, that's his real name," said Art with a merciless smirk. "I'm trying to make a gentleman out of him, so he can live up to it."

"What do other people call you?" Roger asked Whitney.

The scowl eased a little.

"Knuckles!"

Roger grinned.

"That's more like it!" he said, and as he turned and went down the steps Knuckles almost grinned back at him.

For a while Inspector Tearle simply walked around the grimy streets of Burgessville, letting his nerves unravel after his experience — and glorying in it. He could hardly wait to report to his assistants. Would Shirley and Thumbs ever flip when they heard about this! He had been pushed around by a thug! Could he stretch it so far as to say "roughed up"? He considered this temptation wistfully but decided against it. He didn't really have any bruises to show, except for a scrape he had collected on one shin while being escorted up the stairs. He stopped to pull up the leg of his chinos and look at it proudly. Unfortunately there was little chance of its leaving a scar.

It was quite a while before his mind settled down enough to allow him to turn his thoughts once again to the case of the missing money and to consider where things stood now, in the light of what he had learned; but once he did begin to think about it, new concerns threw a damper on his elation.

For come to think of it, what had he accomplished but to increase the certainty that it was B.J. who was taking the money? And tonight, when the others found out, what was Roger to do? Angel Rose ought to know that even though B.J. had been taking the money he had been doing it for a good cause; and if B.J. didn't say so, Roger would have to, even though he had promised Art . . .

Complications upon complications! Inspector Tearle thought about other cases he had been involved in and sighed.

"This one takes the cake," he told himself. "It really takes the cake!"

Eleven

THE TENT WAS FULL, and so were the collection bags.

"We always have a big night on Saturday," Angel Rose remarked as they carried the bulging bags out to the office. "But don't worry, kids, tonight we'll all count. Leroy, you'd better help, too, otherwise they'll never finish in time because Roger has to mark the money."

Even while Roger was unlocking the drawer and taking out the marking liquid and Shirley was fetching pads and pencils for everyone, Angel Rose and Brother Leroy had begun counting. By the time Roger had established himself at one corner of the table, she had a stack ready for him, with the ends of the bills squared up.

"Here, Roger, mark these."

Holding the stack by the middle, Roger ran the brush down the edges, pressing hard enough to riffle the bills apart as it went.

94

"That ought to do it!" applauded Angel Rose, as he tossed them into the Blessing Box. Brother Leroy waved a stack of bills with a flourish.

"Here you are, Roger! Not as fast as some people, but not too bad."

With three of them counting, the work went along at a good rate, so that before long Angel Rose was able to look around at what was left and say, "We're safe now. We'd better get going, Leroy, the kids can finish up — don't you think, Shirley?"

"Sure, I can count the rest by myself and Roger can mark it."

Angel Rose cast an expert eye over the money.

"It'll run close to twenty-five hundred tonight, if I'm any judge. Well, let's go, Leroy."

They left Roger and Shirley to continue their work, with Shirley's fingers flying at a pace that impressed her brother.

"You'll be able to get a job in a bank after this," he said.

"Quiet, I'm counting," said Shirley. "Here, here's another hundred."

While Roger marked the bills he was thinking hard, and his face wore a dissatisfied frown. It was all a matter of logic, of course. You had two possibilities, A and B. If A was impossible, then it had to be B. If B was impossible, it had to be A.

But what if you didn't like either A or B?

He didn't, but there didn't seem to be anything he could do about it.

"Well, that's it!" Shirley said presently, handing him the odd amount left over. "Seventy-two dollars."

He marked the last bills. She gathered the tallies together and totaled them.

"Angel Rose was right on the button," she announced. "Twenty-four hundred and seventy-two dollars. No wonder she could tell when the count was running short."

Roger tossed the final batch into the box and put the cap on the bottle. While Shirley mixed the bills around, he returned the bottle to the drawer and locked it. Shirley tore off the tally sheets, stuffed them in her pocket, and put away the pencils and pads. Roger glanced around, checking everything, and Shirley peeped through the venetian blinds.

"Lights not out yet. We really did a job."

"Good."

As they waited, Roger was still thinking, thinking, thinking. There was a pattern there somewhere, a repetition of something that he could not quite put his finger on as yet, but —

"There they go!"

The lights were out in the tent.

"Okay, let's get by the door."

An old rule was running through his mind: If the possible is impossible, then the impossible has to become possible. So what if A was impossible, and so was B? If that were the case, then . . .

There had to be a C!

The organ sounded, the "Hallelujah!" rang out. Roger pushed open the door.

"Get going," he said as Shirley jumped outside. "I'll be out in a minute."

And with that he closed the door, leaving her so astonished she almost forgot to run to her hiding place.

Roger had said a minute, but actually it was less than half that before he slipped out and ran to his place behind Angel Rose's camper. As he bellied down in the grass he was full of fierce excitement. There *was* a C, but there was nothing he could do about it yet. The only thing he could do was to let events run their course. It seemed the surest way to get at the truth.

He watched the shadow cross from the tent to the office, right on schedule, and watched it return. And Pete had hardly disappeared into the tent before Shirley joined her brother.

"Roger!"

"Not so loud!"

"Roger, what were you doing in there?"

"I thought of something I wanted to check up on. I can't tell you about it now because I want you to be able to act naturally when the time comes."

"Roger, sometimes I could brain you!"

They joined Thumbs, and Roger had to repeat everything to him, because Thumbs had seen how they left the office one at a time.

"I am *not* being a stinker!" Roger protested when Shirley complained again. "I really can't tell you anything yet because I still don't know exactly what's going on. You'll find out plenty before long, so lay off!"

The crowd had gone home, the cleanup job was finished, and B.J. had given his tally to Angel Rose. The moment had come.

It began when they reported to her. She asked them to come in. She had changed her white robe for a severe black dress she must have felt was suitable for the solemnity of the occasion.

"B.J.'s count was twenty-three sixty-two," she told them, "so it's the same thing again, a hundred and ten dollars short."

A hundred and ten. The amount bothered Roger, but he would have to wait for an answer to that.

"Come on, we'll go over to the office. Leroy's rounding up the men," she said, and led the way. "Soon as he tells them to come, he'll knock on B.J.'s door and ask him to step over."

They had not been in the office long before the men appeared. They shambled inside looking vaguely uneasy, with Pete bringing up the rear.

"Leroy says we're to have a special confab," said Floyd, who led the way. "What's up, Rose?"

"Leroy's getting B.J.," she replied. "They'll be here in a minute. Sit down, boys."

They sat down in a row on one of the bunks, reminding Roger of the three monkeys — Hear No Evil, See No Evil, Speak No Evil. Tonight was not going to be the night for that.

Outside, voices made it clear that the others were on the way. The door opened. B.J. came in first, followed by Brother Leroy.

"Now, what's all this about, Rose?" B.J. asked a bit testily, as though he did not relish having general meetings called by anyone other than himself. He shot a surprised glance at the youngsters. "And what are the kids doing here?"

"They're part of it, B.J. This is important, real important, or I wouldn't have acted this way," said Angel Rose. "I know it must seem to you like I've stepped out of line, but I think you'll understand when you hear what's been going on."

"Well . . ." B.J. sat down on the second bunk, folded his arms, and wriggled the fingers of one hand in a go-ahead sign. "Let's hear it."

"Well, it's just this," said Angel Rose. "B.J., someone's been getting in here lately and taking money from the Blessing Box."

That changed his attitude. Gone was the petty concern for protocol. He looked as hurt as though he had suddenly been struck, and yet he did not look thunderstruck with surprise. Rather, he looked as if a vague dread had crystallized.

"I was afraid of that. I was hoping it wasn't so, but . . ."

Angel Rose did not look surprised, either.

"I knew it was worrying you, B.J." She eyed him intently. "I knew you were getting the feeling the collections were coming up short, just as we did, and trying to tell yourself it wasn't so, the way we did. But now there's no doubt about it — and I'll explain how we know."

She had their full attention.

Twelve

ANGEL ROSE GESTURED toward the youngsters.

"The reason the kids are here is because they've been helping us to find out what's going on. I'll explain more about that in a minute, but first I want to tell you how I really got onto this in the first place."

She glanced at Roger and told him, "Some of this is going to surprise you. I've been holding out on you. I didn't want to tell you everything we knew, because I didn't want to prejudice you. I wanted you to find out whatever you could without having made your mind up beforehand."

Her brilliant blue eyes went back to B.J.

"When Leroy and I got this feeling that someone was getting at the money, at first we didn't see what we could do about it. It had to be happening between the time when we brought those bags out here and put the money in the Blessing Box and when you came out to bless it and count it — but during most of that time Leroy and I had to be in the tent.

"But then I had an idea. I got out my camera, and every night I took a picture of the money in the Blessing Box. You always go to your camper for a minute before you come on over to the office, B.J., so that gave me a chance to slip in and take another picture when the meeting was over.

"Well, those pictures didn't match. Bills that showed up in the first one were gone in the second one, every time. Not bad, huh, Roger?" she said, flashing another glance his way, and he nodded, genuinely impressed. He had never figured Angel Rose for a dummy, but now he felt he was beginning to understand how clever she really was.

"So now we knew money was being taken," she went on, "but we didn't know how much. Finally we did something I know you won't like, B.J., but we felt we didn't have any alternative. One night Leroy and I counted the money."

B.J.'s hand banged flat on the table.

"I *knew* that money had been touched and handled," he declared. "I could feel it!"

"I don't doubt it, and I'm sorry," said Angel Rose hurriedly, "but anyway, sure enough, your count and ours didn't agree."

Now B.J. was staring at her with burning eyes, and it was plain he was trying to reason with himself, trying to talk himself out of being angry.

"Go on, Rose," he said in a gritty voice.

"Well, now where were we? We didn't want it to be just our word there was money being taken — and just about then the Lord brought us to this place where we are now, a place where an old schoolmate of mine came to see me, and brought along her kids, and one of them turned out to be a boy who's a regular detective and has even gotten letters about his fine work from the head of the State Police. And that's what gave me the idea of having the kids help."

All eyes turned toward Inspector Tearle, who failed to accept their scrutiny with the poise he longed for. He could feel his face growing at least pink, if not red. B.J.'s eyebrows shot up. His expression indicated that he did not like the idea of boy detectives but was trying to reserve judgment until all the evidence was in.

On the opposite bunk the three trusted helpers had been looking on and listening with expressionless faces. Their eyes were unsteady, especially Homer's, but then they had never been too steady in the best of circumstances. The cold glances they now wheeled in Roger's direction, however, made their feelings plain: Old associations rendered any reference to the police unwelcome in any form and in any context. Leaning back with his elbows on the built-in cabinet, Brother Leroy was silently

watching everything, and for once not a tooth was showing.

"The *kids*?" said B.J finally. "How have they been helping you in this — this business?"

Angel Rose drew in a breath, then let them all have
the news.

"For the last three nights they've been counting the
money, and every night it's been short."

In the silence that followed, her words seemed to lin-
ger, throbbing in the air. After a pause, she went on.

"So tonight we want to clear all of us and make sure it
hasn't been an inside job. For a starter, let's all show any
money we've got on us, all right?"

Confused glances were exchanged and B.J. said
sharply, "What's that got to do with it?"

"You'll see, B.J. Trust me," said Angel Rose. She had
laid on the table a small purse she was carrying. Brother
Leroy stepped forward to lay a shiny black wallet beside
it.

B.J. grunted, then reached for his hip pocket, pulled
out a worn brown leather billfold, and slapped it down.
Meanwhile the three helpers were fumbling in their
pockets. Floyd brought out a small roll of bills, two fives
and three singles. Homer found a ten-dollar bill and laid
it in front of him. Pete produced an old wallet and took
out two tens and four singles. A glance from Angel Rose
had already sent Roger to the drawer. He returned with
the lamp and plugged it in.

"What's that?" demanded B.J., looking as if he suspected it of being an infernal machine.

"You'll see," said Angel Rose. "If any of this money is from the box, you'll see. All right, who's first?"

"*I'll* be first!" said B.J., shoving his billfold toward her almost scornfully. She opened it without a word, took out several bills, and held them under the lamp. First one end of the bills, then the other; then she turned them over and repeated the process. Nothing showed. Without a word she returned them to the billfold and put it back in front of B.J.

"Who's next?"

Looking at her with the eyes of a poker player dealing a card in a big hand, Floyd shoved his money forward. She put it under the light, returned it, and picked up Homer's ten-spot. Hurrying now, she put the bill under the lamp almost negligently . . .

A violet mark glowed on the edge!

At first they all simply stared, and no one stared harder or with more astonishment than did Inspector Tearle.

Homer! How could it be Homer? Roger had an A, a B, and a C now — but how could that C be Homer?

The watery eyes blinked and finally went to Angel Rose.

"Well, you could have been bluffing," he said mildly. "I had to take my chance."

Angel Rose seemed as surprised as the rest of them,

but she recovered faster. With a sudden, determined movement she put Homer's bill back in front of him, snatched up Pete's bills, and put them under the lamp.

Both of his ten-dollar bills showed violet marks.

Pete's eyes went wide.

"Hey! What —"

A sigh from Floyd interrupted him.

"Now, listen guys, we're going to stick together," he told them. "B.J., we're all three in on this. We figured we were entitled to a cost-of-living raise, but we didn't like to bother you about it, so every night Pete's been taking a ten-dollar bill from the box."

Nobody was watching Roger's face at that point, so nobody noticed how his bewilderment suddenly eased. An important detail had been cleared up for him. It was true that Pete could not have taken a hundred and ten dollars out of the box without his hearing anything, but it was also true that an old pickpocket could have delicately lifted a single bill without making a sound.

"Two nights ago he kept one for himself," Floyd was explaining, "last night he gave one to me, tonight he gave one to Homer. And now it looks like he's also been taking a little bonus for himself, which I guess you can't blame him for, since he was doing all the work."

Angel Rose seized on the point avidly.

"A little extra is right!" she said. "The count has been over a hundred dollars short every night!"

"What?" Pete's voice was shrill. "I ain't never taken

but one ten-spot a night, I *swear* it! Somebody switched that money with what I had in my wallet!"

Angel Rose looked down at him with a sad smile, as much as to say that they still loved him even though they knew him well.

"Now, Pete, let's not hear the old song-and-dance. We know that only two people could have taken that money after the kids counted it, either you or B.J., and it certainly wasn't B.J."

Roger had not realized how hard it was going to be to do what he now had to do. By now he had given them all enough rope to hang themselves; the time had come to act. But it made him a little sick to have to do it.

He stepped forward and directed his remarks to B.J., who was sitting slumped down on the bunk looking as though the world had fallen around his ears.

"Pete's telling the truth, B.J.," he startled them all by saying. "Besides Homer's ten, there's another hundred missing, and those bills of Pete's aren't any part of it. Somebody had an extra key to that drawer. Somebody wanted to make sure Pete was carrying marked money, so somebody marked those bills and then got hold of Pete's wallet and switched them with some he already had."

Roger's unexpected support had taken Pete's breath away, but he managed to croak a few words.

"That's right! I always hang up my coat out in back, where anybody could get at it —"

"Okay," said Roger, without taking his eyes off the Reverend Buddy Joe. "But if you didn't take the missing hundred out of the box, B.J., and Pete didn't take it out of the box, then there's only one place it can be — still in the box!"

With that Roger tipped the Blessing Box toward him, reached inside, dug his fingers into the padded cloth along one edge, and lifted it.

"There! It has a false bottom!" he said, while the others jostled each other for a look at the bills that had appeared underneath it. B.J. and the men did, that is. Angel Rose was as still and white-faced as a marble statue. B.J. gasped and looked up at her with stricken eyes.

"Rose! And you made that box for me with your own hands not two months ago!"

"I wish I'd known that before," said Roger. "You see, I finally remembered every how night, just after the first hundred went into the box, somebody did something to distract our attention so that Angel Rose could flip the false bottom down into place without our seeing her do it. It's what magicians call misdirection."

There was a second or two of high-tension silence, and then Angel Rose cried out a hurried confession.

"It's truè, B.J.! I fixed that false bottom when I was putting on the cloth, and I marked those —"

But before she could finish, Brother Leroy had his arm around her.

"No you don't, Rose. I'm the one who built that box, B.J. I learned the trick from a magician when I was bumming around with a carnival."

Angel Rose looked at him and burst into tears.

"Oh, Leroy! Why couldn't you keep still? What good does it do now for you to lose out, too?"

"Take it easy," he said, patting her shoulder. He looked down at B.J. "We were in it together, all the way. And when we saw that you were catching on that something was wrong, we decided we'd better protect ourselves —"

"We saw a chance to get a little nest egg together and we couldn't resist it. Oh, Pete, can you forgive me?" sobbed Angel Rose, looking across at him. "It was my idea. We were only trying to save our own necks, and you *had* started taking money first, so we . . . we . . ."

Brother Leroy was still looking at B.J.

"What do you want to do, B.J.?" he asked.

B.J.'s eyes bored into his for a moment, then turned away.

"Nothing. Just go, and sin no more," he said, and then added bitterly, "but pack your bags and git tonight!"

Without another word Brother Leroy led the sobbing Angel Rose to the door. Only then did she glance at Roger, and he was surprised to see no hatred in her eyes, but rather something else, a sort of wonder.

"The Lord sent you to me, all right, but he sent an

angel of vengeance, and I got what I deserved," she declared with heartrending conviction.

Then B.J.'s anger took him to the Scriptures.

"A fugitive and a vagabond shalt thou be in the earth!" he thundered, quoting Genesis 4:12.

Angel Rose caught her breath, but managed to reply — with the next verse, Genesis 4:13.

"My punishment is greater than I can bear," she said in a broken voice, and she stepped out into the dark.

When they had gone there was silence while the Reverend Buddy Joe sat gazing toward the door with his face working.

"Oh, the way that girl knows her Bible!" he groaned finally. "It's enough to break your heart!"

He sagged down, looking old, tired, and defeated. All the magnetism was gone, all the charisma, all the confidence.

"Well, I guess this is the end of the road. Five trusted helpers, and every one of them — every last *one* of them had his hand in the till! I've failed. I've failed completely."

Across from him, Homer coughed.

"What about us, B.J.?"

B.J.'s eyes burned across at the men, and he roused himself a little.

"What about you?" He snorted. "If I sent you three packing, you'd all be back on Skid Row in less than a week. Anyway . . . no sir, I haven't failed *completely*," he said, rousing himself yet a little more. "You men stuck together and took your medicine together, and men who can do that can't be all bad, not by a long shot. Besides, who am I to cast the first stone? I know what temptation is — brothers, do I ever know! Every time I pick up a paper and Satan directs my guilty eyes to the sports section and I happen to see where a good horse is running somewhere, I want to step up to the hundred-dollar window and put a bet down so bad I can *taste* it! I have to fight the temptation every day of my life."

He sighed and looked toward the door again.

"And those two, they stuck together, too. But from now on, for them, it's downhill all the way — I can see it as clear as if I were there. They'll drift from one cheap hotel to another, trying to make ends meet, trying sharp tricks because they don't have what it takes to make an honest living, and sooner or later they'll both end up in jail or worse. They're poor, weak creatures, and they can't save themselves without help."

He passed a trembling hand across his face and squeezed his eyes shut, and his lips moved as though he were praying. Then he opened his eyes and looked across at Pete with a strange, beseeching expression, hoping against hope.

"Well, Pete, what do you say?" he asked. "Can you forgive them?"

Pete stared back at him for a long moment. His

Adam's apple bobbed twice as he swallowed. His lips trembled, then firmed.

"I guess I can if you can, B.J.," he said.

It was as if he had touched a lever, or closed a switch. Color and vitality suddenly flooded back into B.J.'s face, strength surged through his body, and once again his eyes were like searchlights. He sprang up and burst through the door, and his booming voice filled the night.

"Now, listen, you two, stop your packing and come out here! You're going to stay right here and do the work of the Lord harder than ever, and I'm going to save your souls if it takes me the rest of my life! You come out here and we're going to kneel down together and do some praying! And tomorrow you're going to stand up in front of me and *get married*!"

Roger listened, bewildered, and turned to stare at the three trusted helpers.

"He's a good man!" he said in a tone of simple wonderment. "He really is!"

Homer sighed.

"Yep, he's a good man, all right, and a good man is a hard thing to live with sometimes," he declared. Then he sighed again. "But I guess we wouldn't live long without him."

Shirley's eyes were shining. "Gee, I hope we get to come to the wedding!"

"I expect we'll all be there," said Thumbs stoutly.

Floyd brightened up long enough to remark, "Well,

anyway, Pete, it's better to forgive than to deceive," and Pete said, "Now, cut that out, Floyd!" out of pure force of habit.

Then Floyd's thoughts turned in another direction, along with his eyes.

"Well, I've seen everything now. A kid detective!" he said, taking a good long look at Roger, who wondered what was coming next.

"Well, I'll tell you one thing, Roger," Floyd went on. "I'm glad I never came up against you in the old days. You'd have nailed me for sure."

It was a remark Inspector Tearle was to treasure every bit as much as those framed letters on his bedroom wall.